Teresa Bateman, author,
with Mrs. Hislop,
October 2004

Traveling Tom and the Leprechaun

by TERESA BATEMAN

illustrated by MÉLISANDE POTTER

Holiday House / New York

A version of this story was originally published in *Cricket* magazine.

Text copyright © 2007 by Teresa Bateman
Illustrations copyright © 2007 by Mélisande Potter
All Rights Reserved
Printed and Bound in Malaysia
The text typeface is Fritz.
The artwork was created with gouache, inks, and collage
(including Irish sheep wool) on Strathmore watercolor paper.
www.holidayhouse.com
First Edition
1 3 5 7 9 10 8 6 4 2

Library of Congress Cataloging-in-Publication Data
Bateman, Teresa.
Traveling Tom and the leprechaun / by Teresa Bateman ; illustrated by Mélisande Potter.— 1st ed.
p. cm.
Summary: A wandering minstrel outwits a leprechaun to win the heart of a princess,
who will only marry a man of daring, intelligence, and humor.
ISBN-13: 978-0-8234-1976-0 (hardcover)
ISBN-10: 0-8234-1976-2 (hardcover)
[1. Fairy tales.] I. Potter, Mélisande, ill. II. Title.
PZ8.B3015Tra 2007
[E]—dc22
2005035641

There once was a king in Ireland who had but one child—a daughter named Kathleen, with hair like autumn leaves and a smile that could charm peat into flames by its warmth.

Many were the lads who fell in love at the first sight of her, yet many were the hearts that were broken, for Kathleen did not wish to marry. She could see in the noblemen's sons around her not a hint of daring, nor a trace of intelligence, nor a spark of humor.

Time passed, and people began to talk. Finally, to silence the gossips, Kathleen vowed she *would* marry; but only a man who could win a leprechaun's pot of gold in a single day's time would win her hand as well. For, as Kathleen herself said, "Everyone knows such a deed requires a daring soul, a keen wit, and a merry heart."

As word spread, men came from near
and far to try for her hand, but they met with no success.
There was but one leprechaun who lived within the valley surrounding
the castle, and he hadn't kept his pot of gold safe these many years by
being careless or inattentive.

Then one day a wandering minstrel came down from the green mountains—
a harp on his back and a skip in his step. He was called Traveling Tom, and it
was said that he loved a challenge above all else.

Traveling Tom went to the palace asking if he might earn a night's lodging by the playing of his harp. As his fingers wandered the strings, he spied the fair Kathleen and, at the sight of her, his eyes sparked and his mouth curved up. Kathleen was shocked at the forward gaze of the minstrel. Still, there was more music in the air that night than could be blamed upon one minstrel's harp.

Hearing of Kathleen's vow, Tom made a vow of his own—to win her over, heart and hand. But first he would have to capture a leprechaun's pot of gold, and for that he would need a plan.

The next morning Tom shouldered his harp and set out for a hillside nearby where wildflowers were scattered across an emerald meadow like stars in a green sky. It seemed the most likely place to find a leprechaun.

Indeed, as he neared the center of the meadow, he could hear the tap of a small hammer pounding tiny nails into a dainty shoe. He rounded a large stone, and there was the leprechaun dressed all in green, almost hidden by the green of the grass.

The wee man looked up.

"Well then, who might you be?"
he asked suspiciously.

Traveling Tom unslung his harp
and found a convenient rock upon
which to perch. He fingered a
gentle chord before answering.

"Just a wandering minstrel," he finally replied.

"And what might you be wanting?" the leprechaun inquired.

"Why, nothing at all," Tom assured him. "All I ask is to share your meadow as I rest my feet."

"Rest is it?" asked the leprechaun. "And here I was thinking you were after my pot of gold."

Tom laughed, and the sound was like church bells on a spring day. "A pot of gold? What use would that be to a traveling minstrel? Gold only weighs down the pockets, and doesn't lighten the heart like a good song can. As a traveling man I've heard some of the grandest tunes from all of Ireland. Would you like to hear some of them?"

Without waiting for an answer, Tom struck up as infectious a tune as ever had been heard. Soon the leprechaun found his toes tapping. When he could stand it no longer, he jumped up and began whirling and high stepping as only the fair folk can.

When at last Tom stilled the strings, the leprechaun collapsed on the grass with a smile of rapture on his face.

"Those are fine tunes you play," he admitted. "And for the dance I'll be owing you a great debt, but not so much as a pot of gold."

"A pot of gold?" declared Tom. "And what use would that be to a traveling minstrel? Gold only weighs down the pockets, and doesn't lighten the heart like a good story can. As a traveling man I've heard the grandest tales from all of Ireland. I'll share one with you."

With that he plunged into the most incredible story of a traveling minstrel who had been turned into a pig by the king of the leprechauns himself for writing a song mocking him.

"Mind you," the minstrel added, "he was handsome, as pigs go; and the only cure for his enchantment was to bathe in the sea off Galway. On his way there, however, a farmer's sow spied him and fell madly in love.

There was never such a sight as that poor minstrel pig running as fast as his trotters could take him to Galway, a lovesick sow close at his heels. At last he came to the sea and plunged in. Imagine the sow on seeing a man rise up out of the water where her beloved had so recently disappeared. It was a grave disappointment. The sow followed the minstrel around for days; and he often awoke with her snout near his face, as if she somehow hoped that a kiss would turn him back into a handsome pig."

The leprechaun laughed until tears of mirth ran down his face. "Indeed, that's a fine tale you tell, and for that, and the music, I'll be owing you a great debt, but not so much as a pot of gold."

"A pot of gold?" Traveling Tom shook his head. "What use would that be to a traveling minstrel? Gold only weighs down the pockets, and doesn't lighten the heart like a fair Irish lass can. As a traveling man I've seen the rarest beauties from all of Ireland. It's a pity you'll never travel and see the world, for I doubt you'll find a fresh song, a new story, or a fair bride, waiting here so weighed down with that pot of gold."

They sat in silence a moment, then the breeze picked up, catching a small feather and blowing it aloft.

"Well." Tom sighed, rising. "It's like that feather I am. Not tied down like you with responsibility, but free to follow the wind to every song it carries, every story it hears, and every skirt it catches hold of. I wish you well with your pot of gold, and I'll be on my way."

"A pot of gold?" The leprechaun stood and rapped Traveling Tom on the knee with his cobbling hammer. "Sure and it's a sorry bargain you've given me. What use is a pot of gold to a traveling leprechaun? For gold only weighs down the pockets, and doesn't lighten the heart like a tune, or a story, or a fair lass. It's *you* who will have to deal with the gold, for it's off I am to see the world."

With that the little man hurried away through the meadow, and in the grass where he had been sitting lay a small pot, entirely filled with gold coins.

Traveling Tom smiled as he picked it up. Now he could claim the hand of the fair Kathleen.

Yet he couldn't help but turn and watch his former companion disappear over the hill, for what he had told the leprechaun had more than a touch of truth in it.